This book
belongs to

_____

MORE FOOD FUN BY
ADAM BESTWICK...

First published in Great Britain in 2016
by Fourth Wall Publishing
2 Riverview Business Park, Shore Wood Road,
Bromborough, Wirral CH62 3RQ

Copyright © Fourth Wall Publishing 2016

'The Bean Machine' ISBN: 978-1-910851-21-0

Printed in China.

fourth wall
publishing

THE BEAN MACHINE

Adam Bestwick

PLEASE
SELECT_

BEANS, beans are the musical fruit,
(the more you eat, the more you toot!)
but here's a tale of a boy named Jack,
who munched on beans with every snack,
in tomato sauce so thick and sweet,
these orange things were his favourite treat,
so here it is in all its glory–
an alternative Jack and The Bean story...

This is Jack and he eats beans for breakfast, lunch and dinner.
If munching beans became a sport, he'd definitely be the winner!
By day, by night and candle light, he'd devour them with a guzzle.
Jack even had his favourite beans on a jigsaw puzzle!

He ate...
Beans on toast (he loved the most)

...and beans on peeled bananas.

...Beans while watching television
(sat in his pyjamas!)

And when Jack reached
the bottom of
his little baked bean tin,
he'd simply ask for
"more beans please"
and wipe sauce off his chin!

Jack's Mum and Dad took it in turns
and came up with a plan,
to heat beans in the microwave
and warm them in a pan.

Jack liked them hot for breakfast,
and cold by afternoon,
he'd eat them from the fridge at night
with his favourite spoon.

But soon there was a problem – an issue with Jack's snack.
A tower of tins had filled the bins and soon began to stack!
The trash was overflowing, and bags were piling high.
The kitchen was an utter mess, and Mum began to cry!

Meanwhile Jack ate...
Beans with noodles, apple strudels

...beans in bowls of stew.

...Beans on ham
(and stirred in jam)

...and even
on the loo!

And when Jack reached
the bottom of
his little baked bean tin,
he'd simply say
"I'd like some more" and
wipe sauce off his chin!

To get rid of the rubbish,
Dad hired a massive van,
and drove to the Recycling Centre,
to get rid of our cans...

But back at home Jack's love for beans just didn't look like stopping...
and as he made more piles of tins – Mum just kept on shopping!

Jack ate...
**Beans on cake
and in milkshake...**

...and beans on ravioli.

...On lemon drops
and lollipops
and beans on
macaroni!

And when Jack reached the bottom
of his little baked bean tin,
he'd smile and say "got anymore?"
and wipe sauce off his chin!

Skips at the Recycling Centre,
were full and piled up high,
and a pyramid of bean cans
was stacked up to the sky!...

...At home in Jack's back garden,
a 'metal mountain' grew,
while Mum and Dad just panicked,
and didn't know what to do.

Meanwhile...
Beans were warmed in pots and pans
that Dad was quickly heating,
Mum zapped beans in microwaves
and Jack just kept on eating...

But at the Recycling Centre,
They're struggling with demand.
"We just can't cope with all your cans,
I'm sorry but YOU'RE BANNED!"

Then...
The 'metal mountain' tumbled – and with a clattering sound...
cans fell on cars and scooters
as they CRASHED down to the ground!
They littered ponds and flattened bikes and bent a garden gate,
it left the neighbour's gardens in such an awful state!

Jack kept eating...

Beans on greens and tangerines,
and beans with
chocolate mousse.

**Beans with peas and
melted cheese...**

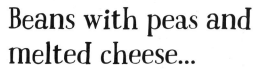

...and plopped in

orange juice!

And when Jack reached the bottom
of his little baked bean tin,
he'd smile and say "I love these beans"
and wipe sauce off his chin!

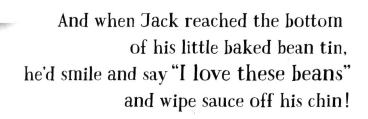

As it got dark Jack noticed,
that things were not quite right,
so staying awake, he made a plan and worked right through the night.
He needed help, and couldn't solve this problem on his own,
so Jack called up his best friend 'Will'
on his tin can phone!

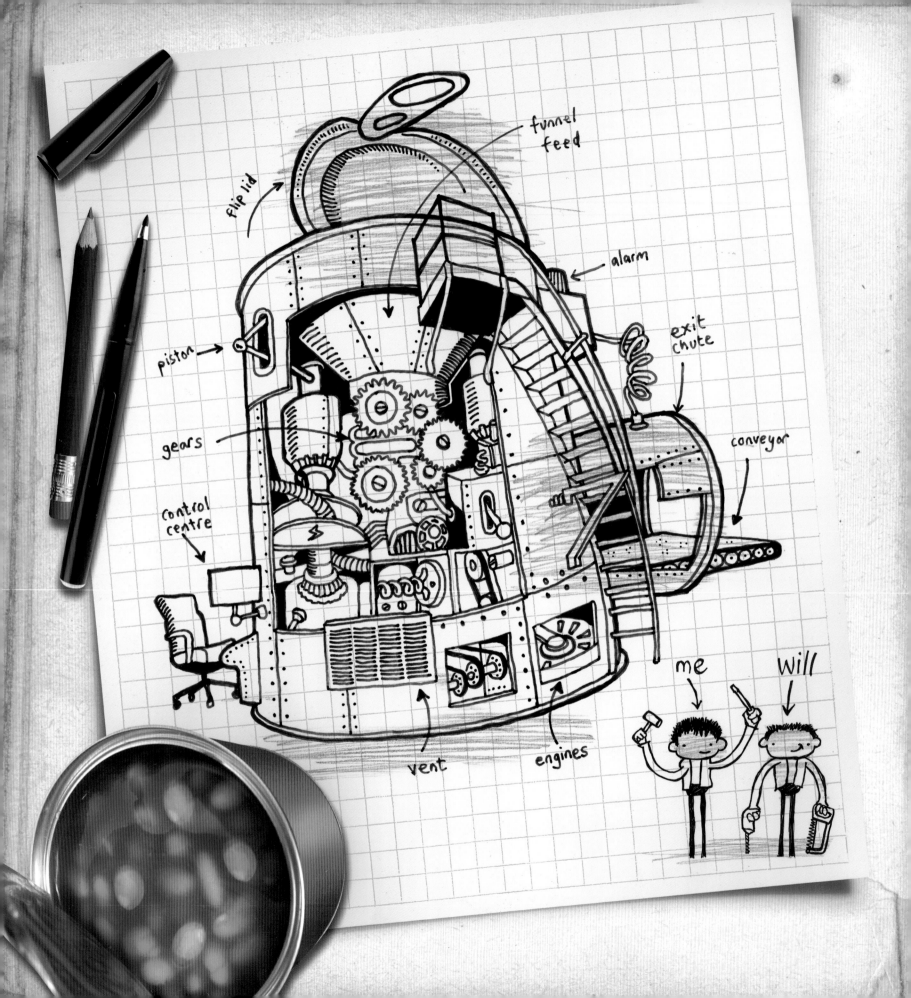

Jack and Will then set to work and using lots of cans,
they cut, they drilled and welded them while following their plans.
Finally, they both stepped back and wiping their hands clean,
Jack announced "Let's call it...

THE AMAZING...

Without delay Will made a start
and loaded in some tins,
"Let's set this Bean Machine to work
and make some metal things!"

So Jack pushed all the buttons, while Will turned a few dials,
then Jack began to access the "Bean Construction Files."
He tapped on the computer and the thing began to shake,
it crunched the cans and noisily, it soon began to make...

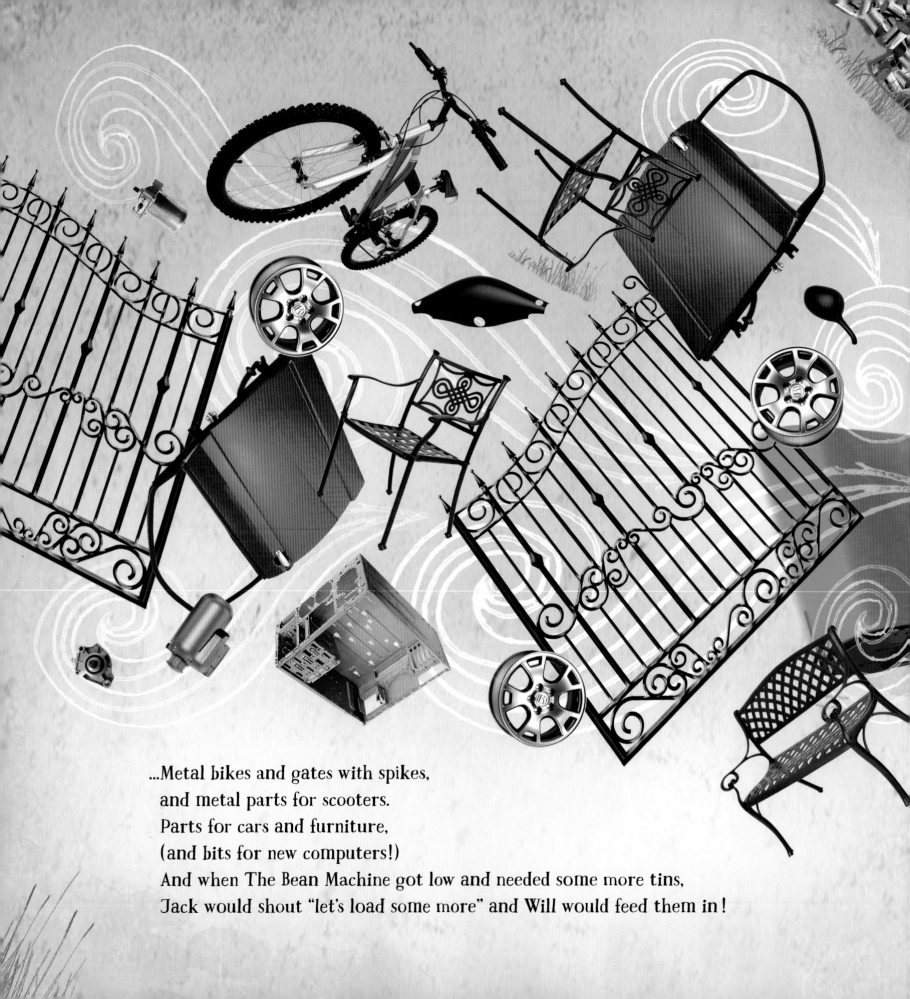

...Metal bikes and gates with spikes,
and metal parts for scooters.
Parts for cars and furniture,
(and bits for new computers!)
And when The Bean Machine got low and needed some more tins,
Jack would shout "let's load some more" and Will would feed them in!

The pile of tins was shrinking
and soon would disappear...
the Bean Machine kept munching cans
as Jack gave a big cheer!...

...With broken things replaced,
and swapped for sparkling new,
Mum and Dad were happy again –
and the neighbours too!

New gates for the Recycling Centre
were delivered on a lorry,
while Jack gave them The Bean Machine
and told them he was sorry.

At home poor Jack was tired,
and settling down for bed,
"I think I need some beans" he said
"to relax my sleepy head..."

"Now where did I put my can opener?..."